Bluebell Woods

Florence's Birthday Wish

For Maddie Shepperd, my number one fan!
~L.N.

With love to Willow xx
~R.H.

STRIPES PUBLISHING
An imprint of Magi Publications
1 The Coda Centre, 189 Munster Road,
London SW6 6AW

A paperback original
First published in Great Britain in 2011

ISBN: 978-1-84715-190-2

A CIP catalogue record for this book is available
from the British Library.

Printed and bound in China.

STP/1800/0001/0211

10 9 8 7 6 5 4 3 2 1

Bluebell Woods

Florence's Birthday Wish

Liss Norton

Illustrated by Rebecca Harry

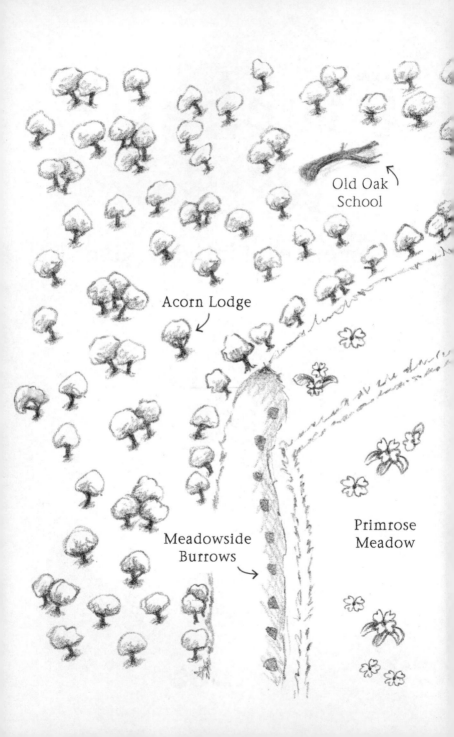

Old Oak
School

Acorn Lodge

Meadowside
Burrows

Primrose
Meadow

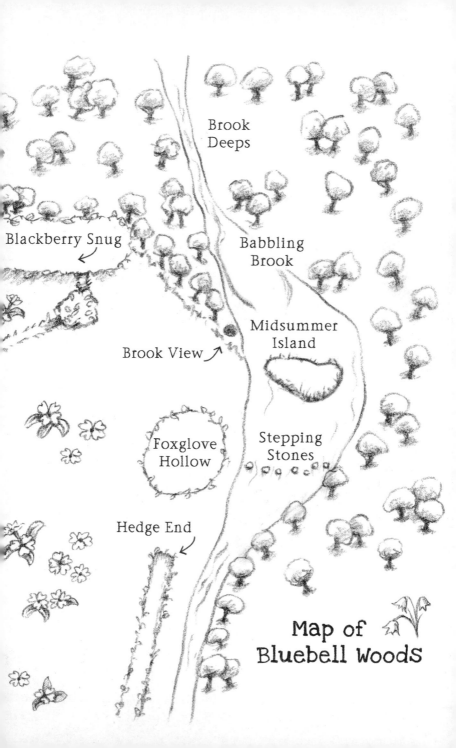

Brook
Deeps

Blackberry Snug

Babbling
Brook

Brook View

Midsummer
Island

Foxglove
Hollow

Stepping
Stones

Hedge End

Map of
Bluebell Woods

Chapter One

"Only a week to my birthday, Rosie!" said Florence Candytuft. She tickled her little sister's soft tummy. Giggling, Rosie batted Florence's ears with her tiny paws.

"Florrie's birfday," she said. "Yippee!"

It was the first sunny day of spring, and Florence and Rosie were stretched out on the fresh grass.

Mrs Candytuft came out of their burrow with her feather duster. She shook it out. "How do burrows get so dirty?" she exclaimed.

Bluebell Woods

"Do you want a hand?" asked Florence, hoping her mum would say no. She didn't want to be indoors brushing away cobwebs on such a beautiful day.

"No, thanks," said Mum. "Having you look after Rosie is the best help of all."

"Can I show you my new skipping step?" Florence asked. She picked up her skipping rope and began to

skip, twisting and untwisting the ivy-stem rope with alternate jumps.

"That's clever," said Mum. "Did you make that up yourself?"

Bluebell Woods

Before Florence could reply, her squirrel friend, Evie Morningdew, came racing along the path that ran past Meadowside Burrows. Her bushy red tail swished to and fro with excitement.

Honey Pennyroyal, a wood mouse, was close behind. "Quick!" she squeaked. "Nat's awake!"

"At last!" Florence cheered. Their friend Natalie Hollyhock, a hedgehog, had been hibernating all winter. "Can I go to visit Natalie, Mum?"

"Oh, Florence," her mum tutted. "You said you'd look after Rosie."

"Yes, I know, but… Oh, please?" she begged. "I haven't seen her for months."

"All right," said Mrs Candytuft, "but I'll need you home in time for lunch.

And could you pick some wild garlic flowers while you're out?"

"For your yummy carrot and garlic soup?" asked Honey, licking her lips.

"That's right," said Mrs Candytuft.

Honey looked at her hopefully. "If you need anyone to try it out…"

"I'll bear you in mind, Honey." Mrs Candytuft laughed. "Now, are you girls going to see Natalie or not?"

Florence nodded. Clutching her skipping rope, she kissed Rosie's pink nose. "See you later, tiddler."

Florence, Evie and Honey charged down the path. At the end of the row of burrows the path bent to the right and cut across a corner of Primrose Meadow. The field was thick with golden flowers.

Evie slowed down a little so Honey
could keep up. "It feels like spring's really
here now Nat's awake."

"I wish she could be with us all
winter," said Florence. "It's not the same
without her."

On the far side of the meadow, the
path ran underneath a hazel bush. As they
reached it, the branches above them
began to shake. "What's that?" Honey
gasped. Suddenly, Albie, one of her twin
brothers, plopped down beside them in a
shower of catkin pollen.

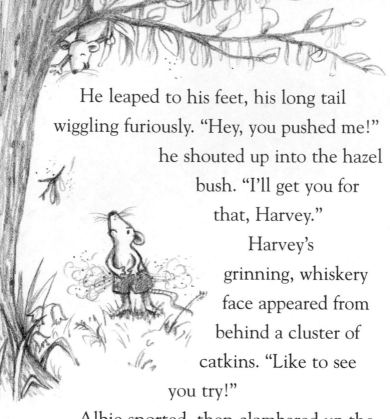

He leaped to his feet, his long tail wiggling furiously. "Hey, you pushed me!" he shouted up into the hazel bush. "I'll get you for that, Harvey."

Harvey's grinning, whiskery face appeared from behind a cluster of catkins. "Like to see you try!"

Albie snorted, then clambered up the trunk.

"Brothers, honestly!" cried Honey.

"At least he didn't hurt himself," said Florence.

"Or land on us!" Evie added.

Behind the hazel bush was the wide bramble thicket where Natalie lived.

12

Taking care to avoid the thorns, they pushed through the thick tangle of arching blackberry canes until they reached Natalie's cosy, round nest, Blackberry Snug.

"Hello! Is anyone there?" Honey called.

"In here," Mrs Hollyhock called back.

They scurried down the entrance tunnel to the kitchen, where Natalie and her parents were tucking into bowls of steaming wild oat porridge.

"Nat! We've missed you *soooo* much!" Honey squealed, flinging her arms round her friend. "Ouch!" She drew back hurriedly, rubbing her paws. "Your spines are sharper than ever."

"Sorry!" Natalie giggled.

"We wouldn't have you any other way," said Florence, squeezing Natalie's paw.

"Can you come out to play?" Evie asked.

Natalie gobbled the last of her porridge. "Is that OK, Mum?"

"Of course it is," said Mrs Hollyhock. "But stay away from Brook Deeps. It'll be dangerous after all the winter rain."

"I will," Natalie promised. Brook Deeps was the narrowest and deepest part of the Babbling Brook.

The friends scampered back up the tunnel and into the fresh air. Natalie stretched and took a deep breath.

"I love spring," she said. "Everything smells so new."

"What shall we do?" asked Evie.

"Play on the Stepping Stones?" Honey suggested. The Stepping Stones crossed the Babbling Brook at its widest point.

"Or we could play skipping games over in Primrose Meadow?" said Florence. "I've got a new step to show you."

"Nat should choose," said Evie.

"Skipping games, then," said Natalie. She beamed at her friends. "It's so good to see you all again. What have I missed?"

"Snow, snow and more snow," said Evie.

"It's a wonder we didn't all freeze!" Honey added, shivering.

"But we had fun, too," said Florence.

"That snowmole we made!" Evie laughed. She lowered her voice and glanced round cautiously. "When it was finished it looked exactly like Mr Hazelgrove." Mr Hazelgrove was their teacher. "It even had that funny little tuft of fur on the back of his head."

"I wish I could've seen it." Natalie giggled. "If only I could stay awake one winter."

"Never mind," said Florence. "At least you haven't missed my birthday. It's on Saturday and I'm planning a picnic at Foxglove Hollow."

"That sounds fun!" said Honey.

Natalie nodded. "I love picnics!"

"I haven't asked Mum and Dad about it yet," said Florence, as they reached Primrose Meadow. "I hope they say yes." She shook out her skipping rope. "Right, who wants to go first?"

They took turns skipping in pairs, arms
linked and each holding one handle of the
rope. Then Florence demonstrated her
new step. By the time the sun was almost
directly overhead everyone had learned
it. "I have to go," Florence sighed. "I
promised I'd be back by lunchtime, and
I've still got to pick some garlic flowers."

"We'll come with you," said Evie,
taking Florence's paw. "I know just the
place for wild garlic."

Bluebell Woods

When Florence arrived home with the starry, white garlic flowers, Mrs Candytuft was scrubbing the kitchen floor with a teasel brush. "Perfect." She smiled. "I'll start the soup straight away."

Rosie came toddling into the kitchen and Florence scooped her up and gave her a hug. "Will Dad be home for lunch?" she asked.

"No, he's out looking for sheep's wool," her mum replied. "He won't be back till late." Mr Candytuft made knitted blankets and was often away searching for scraps of wool that had been caught on thorn bushes. "Why don't you take Rosie outside and I'll call you when it's ready."

Florence put Rosie down. "You know it's nearly my birthday, Mum," she said.

Bluebell Woods

"Do you think I could have a picnic? At Foxglove Hollow?"

"I'm not sure…" her mum began.

"It would be brilliant fun," said Florence. "And I could help with getting everything ready."

Mrs Candytuft scratched her nose thoughtfully. "I'll talk to your dad. Then we'll see."

Florence felt a stab of disappointment. "We'll see" usually meant "no". But it was no use making a fuss. This was a busy time, and her mum hadn't actually said no, so perhaps there was still a chance. She touched her tail three times for luck and took Rosie out to play.

Chapter
Two

Next morning, Florence and her friends
met up on the edge of Bluebell Woods.

"Dad wants me to collect twigs for his
brooms," Natalie said.

"We'll help," Florence offered.

"I hoped you'd say that," said Natalie,
grinning. She handed each of them a
basket.

Evie picked up a stumpy twig. "Is this
one OK?"

"Perfect," said Natalie.

They worked their way through the

woods, picking up twigs and chatting as they went. In a clearing they found Albie and Harvey tying fallen twigs together.

"What are you up to now?" Honey tutted.

"Making a raft, if you must know," said Harvey, tying the last twig  in place. "Come on, Albie, let's try it out."

The two brothers picked up the raft and jogged across the clearing. "If you fancy a sail, just let us know," Albie shouted as they vanished into the undergrowth.

Honey snorted. "Go sailing with you?" she called. "You'd probably push us in."

"How did you get on with your birthday picnic plan, Florence?" Evie asked.

21

Florence sighed. "Mum said, 'We'll see' and you know what that usually means."

"Maybe she needs to think about it a bit," said Natalie.

"I suppose," said Florence, "but I know she's really busy at the moment. And it's only six days to my birthday so it's going to be a bit of a rush if we don't start organizing it soon."

Suddenly, Honey let out a yelp. "Oh no, it's raining!" she exclaimed. Her silky brown fur was spotted with drops of water.

Florence looked up at the patches of blue sky between the branches. "It can't be," she said. "There aren't any clouds."

"I'm wet too," said Natalie, shaking drips from her spines.

Suddenly, they heard laughter in the bushes, then the scuffling of feet.

"Someone squirted us on purpose," Honey cried. "After them!"

Throwing down their baskets, the friends gave chase. Florence was soon ahead of her friends, but Honey and Evie weren't far behind. Natalie was struggling along, clambering awkwardly over jutting tree roots. "You two go on," Evie panted. "I'll wait for Nat."

Florence and Honey kept running. They could hear rustling ahead, but whoever it was stayed out of sight under the low-growing bushes.

"Stop!" Honey shouted.

Florence jerked to a halt. "What's up?" she asked breathlessly.

"Listen."

Bluebell Woods

Florence pricked up her long ears and caught the splash of fast-flowing water. "We're almost at Brook Deeps," she said, as Evie and Natalie caught them up.

"I don't mind risking it," said Evie. "If we're careful and stay away from the edge, we should be OK."

Natalie shook her head. "It's too dangerous. And I promised Mum I wouldn't go near there."

"None of us should," said Florence.

"So those rotten water squirters have got away!" said Honey, stamping her foot.

"I wonder who it is," said Florence. "They must be good swimmers if they're not scared of Brook Deeps."

"Lily and Luke Willowherb are the best swimmers I know," said Evie. They were otters who lived in a cosy hole, Brook View, right beside the Babbling Brook.

"And they're always up to something," Honey added. "Do you remember when they came to school filthy because Luke had started a mud fight with the weasels?"

"Yes," said Evie. "I bet it was them. Why don't we pay them a visit?"

"I can't," Florence sighed. "I have to get home to babysit Rosie."

"And I'll have to go back for my dad's twigs," said Natalie.

"You'll never carry all those baskets on your own," said Evie. "Honey and me will give you a hand."

"But what about Luke and Lily?" Honey demanded.

"We'll talk to them at school tomorrow," said Evie.

"See you then," said Florence, and headed for home. She loved playing with Rosie, but she couldn't help feeling that she was missing out when her friends went off without her.

Evie, Natalie and Honey walked back the way they'd come. "What a shame Florence had to go," said Natalie.

"Yeah, Rosie's very sweet, but it can't be much fun having to look after her all the time," said Honey. "I hope Florence's mum and dad say she can have her birthday picnic."

Bluebell Woods

Evie stopped suddenly.

"What's wrong?" Natalie asked.

"I've had an idea; why don't *we* organize Florence's birthday picnic?"

"That's a great idea," said Honey. "What do you think, Nat?"

"Brilliant," Natalie agreed. "I can be in charge of the food. I'll bake apple blossom cookies – they're Florence's favourite."

"I'll write out the invitations," said Honey. "My handwriting's neatest."

"And I'll organize some races," said Evie. "Florence loves games."

"A skipping race," said Natalie. "That would be perfect! But first, we need to check with Florence's mum that she's happy for us to organize the party."

"We can do that tomorrow after school," said Evie. "I'm sure she won't mind."

Honey grinned at the others. "This is so exciting! But we'll have to keep it secret. Don't breathe a word to Florence."

"Not a word," Natalie and Evie agreed.

Chapter
Three

Next day, school restarted for the spring term. Natalie, Evie and Honey were already in the classroom when Florence arrived at Old Oak School – a hollowed-out tree.

"Luke and Lily Willowherb aren't here yet," said Evie. "Maybe they feel so guilty about squirting us, they've stayed away."

Mr Hazelgrove strode in. "Welcome back," he said. "Places, everyone."

"The same places as last year?" Honey asked.

Mr Hazelgrove nodded.

Honey groaned. "I'll have to sit next to Harvey again!"

"Bad luck!" Florence laughed. She headed for the back of the class and sat down at her desk between Johnny Beechmast, a mole, and Sophie Chervil, a rabbit who lived close by in Meadowside Burrows. Natalie and Evie were at opposite ends of the next row, and Honey

was right at the front.

Mr Hazelgrove handed out some plants. "These are lily-of-the-valley and wild garlic plants," he said. "Sketch them in your books and note their similarities and differences. This is important because, although they look alike, lily-of-the-valley is poisonous and wild garlic is, of course, delicious."

"Especially in carrot soup," Honey called out. Everyone laughed, except Mr Hazelgrove, who looked at her sternly through his very small eyes.

Everyone set to work, making charcoal sketches of the two plants. Suddenly, Florence noticed Evie writing on a scrap of paper. She folded it in two and passed it forward to Honey.

Honey read it quickly, scribbled something at the bottom then whispered to Monty Hornbeam, the shrew who sat behind her. The note was passed from paw to paw until it reached Natalie. Florence waited for it to come to her.

Natalie wrote something on the note, refolded it and sent it back to Evie.

Bluebell Woods

Florence stared in dismay as Evie glanced at it, then tucked it into her school bag. *Why haven't they passed it to me?* she wondered. She tugged at one ear unhappily. *Why are they leaving me out?*

Mr Hazelgrove marched towards Evie and held out his paw. "I'll have that, thank you."

Horrified, Evie retrieved the note from her school bag. "It seems Evie has something she wishes to share with us all," announced Mr Hazelgrove.

"Sir," Evie said in a panic-stricken voice.

Mr Hazelgrove began to read the note: "'What do you think about—?'" He broke off. "Ah, I see… Well, I won't have notes passed around in class." He scrunched up the note and threw it in the bin.

Florence stared at her work, feeling miserable. Suddenly, a thought struck her – perhaps they'd left her out because they thought she wasn't much fun any more. Even on the day that Natalie had woken up she'd had to rush off to look after her little sister.

Florence made up her mind to show her friends she was still fun, even if she didn't have much time to play.

"How about a game of tag?" Florence asked, when school ended.

"Sorry, Florence, I'm busy," said Evie.

"So are me and Nat," said Honey.

"What are you all doing?" Florence asked, disappointed.

Natalie, Evie and Honey exchanged awkward glances. "Um… This and that,"

Natalie said vaguely.

"Haven't you even got time to go to the Stepping Stones?" Florence asked.

"I've got something really important to do first," said Evie. "But you three could go." She winked at Natalie and Honey. "I'll see you there in ten minutes."

Florence, Honey and Natalie headed for the Babbling Brook. "What was in that note?" Florence asked.

Honey stared at her. "Note?"

"The one you were passing in class."

"Oh, that note," said Honey.

"It was nothing," Natalie said quickly. "Just … er…"

"A funny picture of Mr Hazelgrove," Honey said. "We couldn't pass it to you cos he was prowling around. Isn't that right, Nat?"

"Yes…" agreed Natalie. "Oh, doesn't Foxglove Hollow look lovely!"

Foxglove Hollow was a wide, grassy dip close to the Babbling Brook. In summer foxgloves bloomed here, but now the ground was dotted with clumps of purple violets. "This will be perfect!" said Honey, as they crossed it.

"Perfect for what?" Florence asked.

Honey's paw flew to her mouth. "Nothing," she said. "I was just…"

"These violets," said Natalie. "They'll be perfect for making pressed flower pictures. That's what you meant, wasn't it, Honey?"

Honey nodded furiously.

Florence was puzzled. Natalie was always making things, but Honey had never shown any interest in pressed flower pictures before.

Bluebell Woods

Meanwhile, Evie ran to Florence's house. Mrs Candytuft was outside, sweeping the doorstep. "Hello, Evie," she said. "Where's Florence?"

"Playing on the Stepping Stones with Nat and Honey," Evie said. "But I wanted to ask you about Florence's birthday picnic. Can me, Nat and Honey organize it?"

"That would be wonderful," Mrs Candytuft said gratefully. "I'm so busy at the moment I was worried I wouldn't have time to plan things. Is there anything I can do to help?"

"You could make some carrot cakes. They're yummy."

"Of course. Anything else?"

Evie grinned. "Keep Florence busy so we've got time to get everything sorted. We want the party to be a surprise."

"I'm sure I can manage that," said Mrs Candytuft, with a smile.

Florence was halfway across the Stepping Stones when Evie arrived. As she jumped from the fourth to the fifth stone, her foot slipped into the cold water. "Botheration!" she exclaimed.

"Bad luck!" Honey called. "My turn."

"Wait, Honey," said Evie, grabbing her arm. She beckoned Natalie over, then lowered her voice. "Florence's mum says we can organize the picnic!"

"Great!" whispered Honey.

"We'll have to start planning," said Natalie.

Florence hopped over the last few stones to the opposite bank, and turned to look behind her. "What's the hold-up?" she called.

"Nothing," Honey called back. She performed a dainty pirouette, then sprang across the stones like a ballerina.

Natalie crossed the Stepping Stones, stopping on each one to peer into the water, then Evie bounded across after her.

"This time let's cross without waiting for the one in front to finish," suggested Florence.

"I'll go first," Honey said. She set off, followed by Florence, Evie and Natalie.

As she reached the last stone, two jets of water squirted out of a bush and hit her tummy. Honey screamed. She wobbled dangerously on one foot, then splashed down into the water.

"Look at me!" she spluttered, struggling to her feet. "I'm soaked!" She waded to the bank and climbed out, shaking water from her whiskers.

Her friends hurried across the stones. "Do you want to go home?" Florence asked. Honey nodded miserably.

Bluebell Woods

Honey's nest, Hedge End, was not far from the Stepping Stones. The entrance hall was woven from grass stalks, and a tunnel led underground to a cosy living room, four bedrooms, a kitchen and a well-stocked larder.

The friends piled into Honey's bedroom, a neat, circular room with polished earth walls. Florence pulled a blanket off Honey's bed and wrapped it round her shoulders. "Is that better?" she asked, but Honey wasn't listening.

"Where's my nest?" she gasped. "The one I wove out of straw for the wooden bird my grandpa carved."

The bird lay on the table beside her bed, but the nest was gone.

"When did you last see it?" asked Florence.

Honey frowned. "I don't know. I was playing with it the day before yesterday."

"Let's see if we can find it," Natalie suggested. She peered underneath the bed, while Florence and Evie rummaged through drawers, but there was no sign of the nest.

"I bet Harvey and Albie took it," said Honey crossly. She stomped out of the room and almost bumped into her older sister, Hattie. "My nest's gone," she complained.

"It's this spring cleaning," said Hattie. "Things get moved and then put back in the wrong places. Mum lost a bucket yesterday."

"It's brothers, not spring cleaning," Honey grumbled. She opened the door of Harvey and Albie's room, then shut it again hurriedly. "What a mess! We'll never find it in there. But just wait till they get back!"

They went into the kitchen, and Honey warmed some damson cordial.

"We need to track down these squirters and teach them a lesson," said Evie. "I still think it's Luke and Lily."

"Maybe they'll be at school tomorrow," said Honey. "And we could ask if anyone else has been squirted too."

"Good idea," said Florence, draining her cup. "I've got to go and look after Rosie for Mum," she said. "Worst luck! See you all tomorrow."

As soon as she'd gone, Evie turned to the others. "I can't stay now, but we need to get planning. How about meeting up after school tomorrow?"

"You can come here," said Honey.

"Perfect!" Evie and Natalie agreed.

Chapter Four

Next day, Evie and Natalie went home with Honey after school to plan Florence's picnic. Luckily, Mrs Candytuft had told Florence to come straight back so there was no chance of her finding out what they were up to.

"Nobody at school's been squirted," said Honey, as they walked along. "I asked everyone."

"I did too," said Evie. "It's just us."

Natalie frowned. "I wonder why."

They arrived at Honey's house and

went into the kitchen. "Let's start with the food," Evie said. She took a sheet of paper out of her school bag.

"Apple blossom cookies," said Natalie. "They're Florence's favourite."

Evie wrote it down.

 "And elderflower jelly," said Honey.

"Dandelion bread,"  Evie suggested. "And Florence's mum's going to make carrot cakes."

"And there'll have to be a birthday cake," Natalie said.

"It should have pink icing," said Honey. "Pink's my favourite colour."

"But it's not your birthday," Evie pointed out. "It's Florence's favourite colour that matters. And she likes purple."

"Purple icing, then," said Natalie hurriedly, before Honey could say anything else. She pulled a sheaf of pale pink paper out of her school bag. "I made this last summer out of birch bark and dog rose petals. I thought it might do for the invitations."

"Perfect!" Honey exclaimed. She sat down at the table. "I'll start writing them now. What shall I say?"

"Hold on. First let's make a list of everyone we're inviting," said Evie.

"There's all of us, for a start," Natalie said. "And Florence and Rosie." Honey wrote down the names, then added Mr and Mrs Candytuft.

"We should invite everyone from school," said Honey. "Except Harvey and Albie."

"We can't leave them out," said Natalie. "It's not fair."

"They'll only muck about," said Honey.

"Even so, they'll have to come," Natalie said. "They're your brothers."

"Don't remind me," said Honey.

"Can Reggie come?" asked Evie. He was her little brother.

"Of course he can," said Natalie. "How many's that, Honey?"

Honey counted the names. "Seventeen. So, what should the invitations say?"

"'Please come to Florence's surprise birthday picnic at Foxglove Hollow this Saturday lunchtime. RSVP: Honey, Natalie and Evie,'" suggested Evie.

"'Surprise' should be in capital letters so they know not to tell Florence," Natalie added.

Bluebell Woods

Honey started writing the invitations. "We won't be able to hand them out at school," she said. "Florence might see."

"We'll deliver them to everyone's homes, then," said Evie.

"But what will we say if we bump into Florence?" Natalie asked.

"I'll say I'm delivering letters for my mum," Honey said.

"Good idea," said Natalie.

Evie made a list of races while she waited for Honey to finish the invitations. "We can have a running race, a skipping race and a three-legged race," she said. "I'll find some prizes for the winners."

"That's everything planned, then," said Natalie.

"And this is the last invitation," said Honey. "Let's get delivering, and then we can pick some blossom for the cookies."

Florence was helping Mum spring clean the linen cupboard when Dad arrived home. "It's been a good day – I found lots of wool," he said, putting down his bulging sack. He picked up Rosie and turned her upside down then swung her up again until she squealed with laughter.

"How was school, Florence?" asked Mr Candytuft, as he set Rosie on her feet. "Did you learn how to tell a newt from a daddy-long-legs?"

Florence laughed. "I already know that, Dad."

Mr Candytuft ruffled her ears. "Didn't I tell you Florence was a genius, Trudy?" he said to Mrs Candytuft. "She'll be able to tell a stag beetle from a worm before long."

"Really, Charles!" said Mrs Candytuft, smiling. "Why don't you go and put that wool away in your workroom?"

Florence watched her dad disappear down the tunnel. "Have you talked to Dad about my birthday picnic yet?"

Mrs Candytuft sighed. "I'm really sorry, Florence, but we just haven't got time to organize a big party for you this year. I hope you're not too disappointed."

Florence felt a lump growing in her throat. "No," she said, trying not to sound too upset. "It's OK."

Suddenly, through the window, she
caught sight of Evie, Honey
and Natalie hurrying
past. Florence
quickly swept out
the empty
cupboard, then
helped Mum pile
everything back inside.
"Can I go out now, please?"
she asked, desperate to join in with
whatever her friends were doing.

"Off you go," said Mrs Candytuft. "But
make sure you're home in time for tea."

Florence dashed outside and ran along
the lane in the direction her friends had
taken. As she reached the far side of
Primrose Meadow she dived under a
clump of cow parsley and almost bumped

into Natalie, who was giving a pale pink letter to Johnny Beechmast at the entrance to his tunnel. "What's that?" she asked, as Johnny whisked the letter out of Natalie's paw and darted indoors.

"Er ... a letter," said Natalie. "From my mum."

"Why's your mum writing to Johnny's mum?" Florence asked.

"I ... I don't know."

They walked round the corner together and found Evie holding another pink letter. "Hi," she said. "I'm just ... um ... delivering a letter for my mum."

Florence was puzzled. "Your mum's started letter writing, too?"

"Looks like it," said Evie, darting an anxious glance at Natalie.

Honey came out of a hole near the end of the hedgerow. She was carrying a bundle of letters and hurriedly tucked them behind her back. "Hi, Florence!"

"What are all those letters?" asked Florence.

"My … um… My mum asked me to deliver them."

Florence stared at her in astonishment. "Your mum wrote all of them?"

Honey laughed nervously.

"Do you want a hand delivering them?" Florence asked.

"No!" Honey squeaked. "No, thanks."

Florence looked at her friends anxiously. *They're leaving me out again*, she thought. They'd walked right past her front door without calling for her. And they kept looking at each other as though they didn't want her there.

"I'm sorry I haven't been able to play much lately," she said. "My mum seems to need loads of help at the moment. And there's Rosie to look after too. And…" She tailed off, close to tears.

"We're going to pick apple blossom," said Evie, putting her arm round Florence. "Why don't you come with us?"

"Evie!" Honey and Natalie cried, dismayed.

"It'll be quicker if Florence helps," Evie said, frowning at them.

Florence flashed her a grateful smile. *At least Evie still wants me around*, she thought. But it was clear Honey and Natalie didn't.

Chapter Five

Natalie was up early next day, baking apple blossom cookies for Florence's picnic. As she put the last tray of cookies in the oven, Evie and Honey arrived carrying a bulging sack. "We've brought the elderflowers for Florence's jelly," Evie said, tipping them out on the table. "How's the cooking coming along?"

"The cookies are baking now," said Natalie. "I'll make the jelly and the birthday cake after school."

"Great!" said Evie. "And I'm going

into Bluebell Woods tomorrow to find some prizes for the races."

Mr Hollyhock came into the kitchen. "Did somebody just mention jelly?" he asked hopefully.

"I haven't made it yet." Natalie laughed. "And anyway, Dad, it's for Florence's picnic."

"Are you ready for school, Nat?" asked Honey. "We really should be going."

Natalie opened the oven door a whisker and peeked in. "I'm ready, but the cookies aren't. I hope they hurry up."

"I'll take them out for you," her dad offered.

"Are you sure?" Natalie asked.

"Absolutely," said Mr Hollyhock. "Now off you go."

"Wasn't it horrible yesterday, having to lie to Florence about the invitations?" Natalie said, as they hurried to school.

"She was really upset," said Evie sadly. "I think she thinks we don't like her any more. That was why I asked her to come with us to pick apple blossom."

"But we can't have her around while we're doing things for her picnic," said Honey. "It would spoil the surprise!"

"I know, but she's so miserable," Evie said. "Maybe we should just tell her about it now and let her help."

"No way!" Honey said. "We've told everyone it's a surprise party. We can't change it now."

Bluebell Woods

"But if it's making her unhappy…" said Evie. "What do you think, Nat?"

"I sort of agree with both of you," replied Natalie. "Florence did look upset yesterday, and I hated lying to her. But she'll love having a surprise party and she's bound to forgive us when she realizes what it was all about."

"So you don't think we should tell her?" said Evie.

Natalie shook her head. "No. It's only for another three days."

Florence was already at school when Honey, Natalie and Evie arrived. *They've walked here together, without me*, she thought glumly. Before she could ask them why they hadn't arranged to meet up with her too, Mr Hazelgrove appeared.

"I have a treat for you," he announced.

Bluebell Woods

"A mushroom-foraging expedition to the far side of Bluebell Woods. It's part of our poisonous plant topic. Mushrooms and toadstools can easily be confused. The outing will take place this Saturday."

Honey gasped in dismay. "I'm busy on Saturday, sir," she called out.

"So am I," Evie said.

"And me," said Natalie quietly.

Florence felt tears prick her eyes. They were doing something together, she was sure of it, and they hadn't asked her. She was certain now that her fears had come true. They didn't want to be friends any more.

Bluebell Woods

"Dear me," said Mr Hazelgrove. "Who else can't come on Saturday?"

A forest of hands shot up.

"Then we will postpone our trip until the following Saturday."

It's my birthday, Florence thought sadly, *and I'm the only one with nothing to do.*

The apple blossom cookies were burned. Natalie could smell them before she, Evie and Honey even entered her nest. She ran down the hall. The tray of blackened cookies was on top of the stove. "I'm so sorry, Nat," said Mr Hollyhock, putting his head round the door. "I forgot all about them. But I could make something else instead. What about acorn biscuits?"

"No, thanks, Dad," Natalie said. "These cookies are Florence's favourite. We'll just have to pick some more apple blossom." She turned to Evie and Natalie. "We can't pick the rest of the blossom from the tree in the woods or there'll be no apples for the winter. We'll just have to pick it from the tree near Florence's burrow."

"I hope she doesn't spot us," said Evie, "or she'll be more upset than ever."

They grabbed a bowl and set off. "How are we going to keep Florence busy while we're getting things ready on Saturday morning?" Natalie asked.

"I've been thinking about that," said Evie. "What if I take her into Bluebell Woods searching for honey, and get her lost, accidentally on purpose?"

"We could have a signal," Honey said

excitedly. "I'll make a cuckoo sound when the picnic's set up and that'll be your signal to bring Florence back." She cupped her paws round her mouth. "Cuck-oo, cuck-oo."

They reached Meadowside Burrows; Florence lived at the far end, right opposite the crab apple tree. "Let's hope Florence isn't looking out of the window," whispered Nat.

"I'll have a sneaky look," said Honey. She tiptoed along the path to Florence's burrow and peeped in. Florence was in the living room playing skittles with Rosie. She had her back towards the window.

"It's OK," Honey announced in a loud whisper. "If we're quick, we might get away with it."

They scampered across to the tree and
Evie and Honey clambered into the
branches.

Inside the burrow, Florence was
teaching Rosie how to roll the ball at the
skittles. "Yippee!" Rosie cheered as the
skittles wobbled and fell over.

As Florence set them up again, she
noticed a movement in the crab apple tree
outside. Standing up to see better, she
spotted Evie and Honey up in the
branches. They were snapping off blossoms
and letting them drift down to Natalie on
the ground.

"Skittles, Florrie," said Rosie, tugging
at Florence's paw.

"Just a moment, Rosie," Florence said,
fighting back tears.

"Skittles!" Rosie shouted.

"I said just a moment!" Florence snapped.

Mrs Candytuft hurried in. "What's going on?" she asked.

Florence couldn't speak. Tears began to roll down her cheeks.

"Florence, whatever's wrong?" Mrs Candytuft sat in an armchair and pulled her on to her lap.

"It's Evie, Natalie and Honey," sobbed Florence. "They don't like me any more."

Mrs Candytuft hugged her. "Of course they do."

"They're outside picking apple blossom, and they didn't call for me."

"Perhaps they thought you'd be busy," soothed Mrs Candytuft.

"And they're doing something on Saturday," Florence sniffed. She buried her face in her mum's shoulder. "They keep leaving me out because they think I'm no fun any more."

"Of course you're fun," said Mrs Candytuft gently. "And everything will be fine, you'll see." She dried Florence's tears with her hankie. "Now come to the kitchen for some carrot cake. I baked it this morning."

"Rosie, carrot cake?" asked Rosie.

"Yes, Rosie, you can have some too."

"I'm sorry I was cross with you, Rosie," Florence said. She slid off her mum's lap and gave Rosie a kiss, before heading into the kitchen.

"Mum, do you think Granny and Grandpa could look after Rosie tomorrow?" she asked, between bites of cake. "So I can sort things out with Evie, Natalie and Honey."

"Of course. But you really don't need to worry."

"Hello," a voice called from the front door.

"Evie!" gasped Florence. She quickly dabbed at her eyes and cheeks to get rid of any last tears.

"Come in, Evie," Mrs Candytuft called.

Evie came scampering into the kitchen. "Hi, Florence, I'm going into Bluebell Woods to find honey on Saturday. Do you want to come?"

Florence smiled. "Yes, please!"

"Great! I'll call for you straight after breakfast. Bye!" Evie dashed out again.

"There," said Mrs Candytuft. "You see? All that worrying for nothing."

Chapter Six

Next day, Florence found herself behind Luke and Lily Willowherb as she went into school. Luke's hind paw was bandaged and he was limping. "What's happened to you, Luke?" Mr Hazelgrove asked.

"I cut my foot on a sharp stone in the Babbling Brook," he explained.

"When was this?" Mr Hazelgrove asked.

"A week ago," Luke replied. "This is the first time I've been out."

"I've had a cold," Lily said. "But it's better now."

They're not the ones who squirted us then, Florence thought. There was no way Luke could have run away from them with that bandaged foot. And Lily wouldn't have done it by herself. She made up her mind to tell Evie after school.

"You're right," Evie said, when Florence told her later. "But if Luke and Lily didn't squirt us, then who did?"

"I don't know," Florence said

thoughtfully. Over Evie's shoulder, she noticed Honey and Natalie running out of school. "Honey! Nat!" she called. To her disappointment, they kept running and disappeared in amongst the trees.

Florence tugged at her ear anxiously.

"Are you OK?" Evie asked.

"Not really," Florence admitted. She took a deep breath, determined not to cry. "I've been feeling a bit left out lately. You, Honey and Natalie keep doing things without me and—"

"It's only because we're busy," said Evie.

"But we used to be busy together," said Florence. "And now…" A tear trickled down her cheek and she wiped it away quickly. "Mum's taken Rosie to Granny and Grandpa's today. I thought I'd have the chance to play with you all, but now

Honey and Nat…"

Evie hugged her. "I'm here," she said. "I want to play with you."

"That's good," Florence said shakily. "But I wish Honey and Nat would play too."

"They will," promised Evie. "After the weekend, we'll all be together again. Come on. Let's play skipping games."

When Florence went home for tea, Evie raced round to Natalie's house. Honey and Natalie were mixing up a bowl of purple icing for Florence's birthday cake, and the kitchen table was laden with food.

"I haven't got any prizes for the races," Evie groaned, sinking into a chair. "I was going to the woods to find some after school, but Florence was so upset I couldn't leave her on her own. She really thinks we don't like her any more."

"You didn't tell her about her picnic, did you?" demanded Honey.

"No, but maybe I should've done."

"But the party's tomorrow," Honey pointed out. "It would be terrible if she found out now!"

"Well, she hasn't," said Evie. She sighed. "Anyway, I played with Florence instead of looking for prizes. I'm sorry."

"Don't worry," said Natalie. "I'll make some prizes. Everything's almost ready. There's just the birthday cake to finish."

"What about the apple blossom cookies?" Evie asked.

"All done." Natalie pointed out the plate of cookies. "So I'll have time to make prizes this evening."

"That's everything sorted, then!"
cheered Honey. She did a little dance,
tapping her feet and wiggling her tail.
"Oh, I'm so excited I can hardly wait!
Florence is going to love it!"

Chapter Seven

Florence woke early on her birthday. Even though she knew there'd be no picnic, she felt excited. With presents and cards to open and her outing with Evie, it would still be a special day – just not quite as special as she'd hoped. *I wish Honey and Nat were coming, too*, she thought.

Determined not to think sad thoughts, she jumped out of bed and ran into the living room.

"Happy birthday, Florence!" Mum and Dad cried, giving her a hug.

"Birfday, Florrie," said Rosie, holding out a present. Florence tore off the paper and found a teasel hairbrush inside.

"Thanks, Rosie," she said, kissing her. "It's just what I wanted."

Mum and Dad had three parcels for her. There was a honey-hazelnut bar – her favourite! – and a hair slide decorated with shiny, red berries. The third present was wide and fairly flat and it felt squashy. Florence tore it open. Inside was a dress. Usually Florence wasn't interested in clothes, but this was the most beautiful dress she'd ever seen. It was made of purple spiders' silk with a ruffle at the waist and a long, flared skirt. "Oh!" she gasped. "It's gorgeous!"

"We thought you could wear it to the Summer Ball," said her mum.

Florence hugged her. "It's perfect," she said. "Just perfect."

Granny and Grandpa Candytuft arrived with a new skipping rope for Florence. It had beautifully carved red wooden handles. "Thank you!" she cried. "I can't wait to try it out."

Evie arrived just as Florence was finishing her breakfast. She was wearing her party dress, and she had a large yellow bow in her tail too.

"Why are you all dressed up?" asked Florence, looking surprised.

Evie shrugged. "I just felt like it." She handed Florence a parcel. "Happy birthday." Inside was a set of wooden juggling balls.

"Thanks, Evie!" Florence exclaimed. "I've been wanting to learn to juggle for ages."

"Why don't you try on your new dress before you go out," said Mum. "We'd all love to see you in it."

Florence changed into the dress and Mum helped her button it up. Evie clipped the new hair slide between Florence's ears. "Wow! You look lovely!" she cried, stepping back to admire her.

"You do!" everyone agreed.

"Thanks." Florence spun round so the flared skirt swished out. "But I'd better take it off if I'm going to the woods. I don't want to ruin it."

"Can't you keep it on," urged Evie.

Mrs Candytuft smiled. "I think you should, Florence, as it's your birthday!"

Outside the Candytufts' burrow, Honey, dressed in a pink party dress, was hiding behind the crab apple tree, keeping an eye on things. She watched Florence and Evie leave, then tore round to Natalie's house.

Natalie was in the kitchen, wearing her red party dress and a shiny necklace made of dried holly berries. "They've gone," Honey cried. "It's time to start setting up."

"Here are the prizes," said Natalie, shyly handing Honey a box.

Honey looked inside. "These are lovely, Nat!" There was a pressed flower picture in a wooden frame, a purple hair ribbon and two sets of mini skittles. "The ribbon should be the prize for the skipping race because

Florence is bound to win and purple's her favourite colour," said Honey.

"I've got ropes for the skipping race too," Natalie said. "And for the three-legged race." She dropped them into the box. "I hope Florence is pleased."

"Pleased?" Honey cried. "She'll be over the moon! Come on, let's go."

"This way," said Evie. She led Florence along a narrow path through the woods, holding the skirt of her dress up so she wouldn't snag it.

Florence did the same. "I'm glad we don't have to wear party dresses every day," she said. "Imagine not being able to run when you want to."

"I bet we'd get used to it pretty soon," said Evie. "By the way, we should listen out for cuckoos."

"It's too early in the year for cuckoos," Florence said, surprised.

"Yeah, but we might hear one," said Evie. "You never know."

"I haven't seen any bees yet," said Florence, as they went further into the woods. "Are you sure there's a beehive here, Evie?"

"Certain. Keep looking."

Soon they were deep in the woods; the trees grew closer together here, making it cold and gloomy.

"Are we lost?" Florence asked at last.

"No. This path here leads to the wild garlic patch." Evie started down it, then stopped in dismay when the path ended at a thicket of stinging nettles. "That's not right," she muttered. She hurried back the way they'd come and searched for another path. This one wound in and out between clumps of wild daffodils, then stopped abruptly at a fallen tree. "We are lost, aren't we?" said Florence, as they retraced their steps.

Evie frowned. "I think we might be. Really lost!"

Florence laughed. "And on my birthday too. Still, I'm sure you'll find the way home."

"Definitely," said Evie, but she looked worried. "Keep listening for that cuckoo."

"There," Honey said. "We've done a brilliant job!" The picnic food was laid out on a colourful blanket with the birthday cake in the centre.

"It does look good," Natalie agreed.

Guests began to arrive, carrying picnic rugs and presents for Florence. "Spread your rugs somewhere near the food," Honey said. "Florence will be here soon." She turned to Natalie. "Shall I give the signal?"

"That sounds like a good idea." As the guests arrived, Natalie had been ticking off their names on a list. "Here come Luke and Lily. And Florence's mum and dad with Rosie and Florence's cousin, Billy. So we're only waiting for Albie and Harvey."

"Hopefully they won't come," said Honey. She cupped her hands round her mouth and gave the cuckoo call, then

peered into the wood, expecting to see
Florence and Evie come running.

"That's funny," she said, after a few
minutes had passed. "Where are they?"

"You don't think anything's happened
to them, do you?" Natalie asked anxiously.

Honey called again, but there was still
no sign of them. She and Natalie
exchanged worried glances.

Suddenly, Honey was hit by a jet of
water. "The squirters!" she exclaimed.
"After them!"

Bluebell Woods

Leaving the picnic and the guests behind, she and Natalie gave chase. The squirters darted away through Bluebell Woods, keeping under cover just as they'd done before. "Come back!" Honey yelled.

On and on they ran, into the gloomiest part of Bluebell Woods. Coming out from under a bramble thicket, they almost crashed right into Florence and Evie. "Florence, Evie! Quick!" panted Honey. "I've been squirted again!"

Forgetting about keeping their dresses clean, Florence and Evie joined the chase. "I know where we are now," Evie panted. "This path leads back to Brook Deeps."

"We're going to lose them," groaned Natalie breathlessly.

"Not if I can help it," said Florence. She put on a spurt and surged ahead of

her friends. If she could just get in front of
the squirters, she might be able to head
them off. Suddenly, two grinning figures
shot out of the undergrowth. They raced
to the Babbling Brook, jumped on to a raft
and punted away from the bank, laughing.
Florence waited for her friends to catch up.

"We thought you'd caught them," Evie
said when they reached her.

"Afraid not," said Florence. "But I
know who they are."

"Who?" Natalie asked breathlessly.

"Harvey and Albie," said Florence.

Chapter Eight

"I might have known it!" Honey burst out. "Trust those two! And they've got away again."

"Don't worry. I should think we'll be seeing them pretty soon, anyway." Evie laughed, giving Honey a wink.

"Will we?" Florence asked, puzzled.

"Come on," Natalie said quietly. "Let's get back."

"I'll go on ahead," Honey said, winking at Evie and Natalie.

"Why do you keep winking at each

other?" Florence asked, feeling left out again.

"You'll soon see," promised Natalie, squeezing Florence's paw.

Honey dashed to Foxglove Hollow. "Quick, everyone hide!" she cried. "Florence is on her way. Jump out when I count to three."

The guests crouched behind the bushes and waited excitedly for Florence to appear.

They didn't have long to wait. "Here we are," said Evie, leading Florence into Foxglove Hollow. Florence looked round at the rugs and food. "Someone's having a picnic," she said.

"One, two, three!" shouted Honey.

The party guests sprang out of their hiding places. "Happy birthday, Florence!" they chorused.

Bluebell Woods

"It's your birthday picnic, Florence," said Evie.

"What…? How…?" Florence gasped.

"We've been preparing it all week," explained Natalie.

"And then Evie got you lost,

accidentally on purpose, in Bluebell Woods this morning," Honey added. "So me and Nat could set everything up."

"Except there wasn't much 'on purpose' about it," Evie added. "We really did get lost! It was lucky you ran into us."

Honey laughed. "That's why you didn't come when I gave the cuckoo signal! We wondered what had happened to you."

Florence beamed at her friends. "So when you were doing things together and leaving me out, you were really getting everything ready?" she said.

"Of course. Trying to keep it a secret was a nightmare!" Honey said.

"I thought you didn't like me any more," said Florence, "because I had to spend so much time looking after Rosie."

Evie hugged her. "You're our friend.

How could we ever not like you?"

Harvey and Albie appeared, carrying Mrs Pennyroyal's missing bucket and two straws. "I bet those straws are from my nest!" Honey squeaked.

"Might be," said Albie, grinning.

"Then you can jolly well weave it back together again," Honey said. "And, as you seem to like water so much, you can wash up after the party."

"Not likely!" cried Harvey.

"I think Dad might be interested to hear what you've been up to," Honey warned.

Harvey gulped. "You wouldn't!"

"Oh yes, I would!"

The brothers trudged away looking thoroughly beaten.

"Win, Florrie! Win!" squealed Rosie, leaping up and down beside Mrs Candytuft. Florence was in front, twirling her skipping rope expertly, but Sophie and Billy were hot on her heels.

Honey was standing at the finishing line by the holly tree. "Go Florence!" she cried.

Florence put on a burst of speed and reached Honey just a whisker ahead of Billy.

"We have a winner!" exclaimed Honey. "That was brilliant!"

"Thanks," Florence puffed. "What's next?"

"The three-legged race," said Evie. "Will you be my partner, Florence?"

"I'd love to!" said Florence. They tied their ankles together with a rope, then stood up, arms round each other's waists, ready for the race to start.

"Ready, steady, go!" Honey yelled.

The competitors dashed away. As Florence and Evie reached the halfway mark, Evie's little brother, Reggie, and his partner, Oscar Bramble, fell over right in front of them. "Look out!" Florence cried. They tried to swerve, but Evie caught her foot on Reggie's outstretched leg and they tumbled over. Giggling, they sat up and untied the rope.

Evie laughed. "Look who's winning."

Harvey and Albie were way ahead of the others. They charged over the finishing line. "Prizes, please, Honey," they said, holding out their paws.

"Just wait," snapped Honey, scowling. "Would all the winners come and collect their prizes, please," she called.

Florence and Sophie jogged across to her. "First in the running race: Sophie," Honey announced. She gave Sophie the pressed flower picture.

"First in the skipping race: Florence." She handed Florence the ribbon.

"First in the three-legged race: Harvey and Albie," Honey said crossly. She gave them the mini skittle sets, then shook her head as they danced away, whooping with triumph. "Brothers!" she snorted.

After the races, everyone tucked in to the picnic food. Florence sat with her friends. "I can't believe you made all this, Nat," she said, helping herself to her fourth apple blossom cookie. "It's delicious!"

"Thanks," Natalie said shyly. "Don't eat too many cookies. There's still birthday cake to come."

Evie fetched the cake and Mrs Candytuft lit the candles. Then everyone sang "Happy Birthday".

"Are you going to make a birthday wish?" asked Honey.

Florence looked round at her friends and family and realized she didn't need to. "I've got everything I could wish for," she said happily.

She blew out her candles, then beamed at her friends. "This has been the most fantastic birthday ever!" she cried. "And the best bit of all is knowing that we're still friends."

"Friends are for ever," said Natalie.

Evie, Honey and Natalie crowded round to hug Florence. "Friends are for ever!" they all agreed.